About the Author

Fran Hodge studied history at Birmingham University but spent as much time playing hockey there as studying. Her love of sport is shared with her husband and two children but her love of books and seafood is just hers! Her teaching career allows her to pass on her passion for sport and learning, whilst encouraging all children to try an activity that they might carry with them through life.

Eddie the Looked After Lamb

Fran Hodge
Illustrations by Alan Preston

Eddie the Looked After Lamb

Nightingale Books

NIGHTINGALE PAPERBACK

A CIP catalogue record for this title is
available from the British Library.
ISBN 978-1-83875-319-1

Nightingale Books is an imprint of
Pegasus Elliot MacKenzie Publishers Ltd.
www.pegasuspublishers.com

First Published in 2021

Nightingale Books
Sheraton House Castle Park
Cambridge England

Printed & Bound in Great Britain

Dedication

To Tolla with thanks.

Acknowledgements

I would like to thank Alan Preston for his beautiful illustrations and constant help throughout.

Many lambs were born on the farm that backed onto the Tollafields' house in Hertfordshire, in the early spring of 2015. But one lost his mummy before he even got to know her. He was wide-awake, fragile and very scared.

He wasn't able to look after himself but the lucky lamb was found and taken to a new home. He went to live with the Tollafields, not in a field like the other lambs but actually in a bungalow.

It was a lovely home joined in a circle to ten other homes and it backed on to a small garden and a large paddock.

The lamb was looked after by Nicky and Emily Tollafield.

Emily instantly fell in love with the tiny lamb with his black legs and snowy white fleece and decided to call him, Eddie.

Eddie loved his name and his new home. Emily fed him warm creamy milk from a bottle every four hours and then he was cuddled before he fell asleep. He started to get stronger and he felt safe and happy.

Emily had to go off to school some days but Nicky would stay to look after Eddie. Eddie wasn't sure what school was or why he didn't go with her but he did know he looked forward to her coming home so much so they could play in the paddock.

There were other animals around too. There were two dogs, Treacle and Lucy, who were even smaller than Eddie and in the paddock there were horses, Marley and Finn, who Nicky and Emily jumped up on and rode each day.

Eddie enjoyed watching them ride around and playing with Treacle and Lucy but his favourite time was when it was his turn to play with Emily.

She set up obstacles and showed Eddie how to jump. They took it in turns. They gambolled through the different courses which Emily made. They ran and jumped until they were so tired they couldn't run or jump any more.

They would then have a shower before their supper and bed. This was Eddie's special time. He slept on Emily's bed and when it got cold he cuddled under her duvet while she read him stories. His favourite story was the one Emily told him about how he came to live with her.

Sometimes they all got in the car, apart from the horses, and went to a nearby farm. The farmer was very busy looking after all her animals but she always made time to come and say hello and give the Tollafields, including Eddie, a cuddle. Eddie liked it there and made friends with the cows and the big dogs who always seemed happy to see him. But Eddie was happy to get home too and back to his special times again, just with Emily.

Eddie thought he would be with the Tollafields forever but he didn't realise things changed when you grew up. Emily gave Eddie some of her extra special cuddles one day just before she got in a very full car.

Eddie assumed that Emily would be back later but only Nicky came back with an empty car. No Emily.

Nicky seemed very sad too so Eddie cuddled up to her while she explained that Emily had now gone to Exeter to study at university.

"Eddie," she said, "I think it might be better if you go and live on the big farm now with all your friends. Would that be OK?"

Well Eddie wasn't sure he wanted to leave the Tollafields home but it wasn't the same without Emily so maybe it was a good idea, just for a little while. So the next time Nicky went to visit the farm Eddie jumped in the car too but this time when Nicky drove home Eddie stayed at the big farm all by himself.

It felt very strange for the first few days and Eddie missed his first home a great deal. Everyone on the farm was so busy.

He didn't really have any special times with anyone and he did miss that. He knew he was lucky and there was food everywhere so in each new building he popped in he would help himself to some of the food left out, he didn't even have to wait for meal times any more. He could eat whenever he wanted and all the animals were very happy to share with him.

While Eddie stayed at the farm he just ate and ate whenever he wanted and he had no one to go running or jumping with.

Unfortunately, he started to get bigger and bigger. In fact, he grew so big he found it was quite hard to walk at all.

He slept in the stables where it was warm and also where he was near to more food.

Poor Eddie felt tired. He didn't know what to do. All the animals were so kind sharing their food and stables but he did miss Emily and his jumping so much.

Luckily Emily came home for Christmas and rushed over to see Eddie at the farm. He was cuddled up in the warm barn, very close to his ready supply of food. At first she didn't recognise him. When she got close she could see her lamb's beautiful blue eyes. It took Eddie a while to get up, partly because he was enjoying being cuddled so much by Emily but also because it took a lot of effort to lift his large body out from his cosy bed. Emily tried to encourage Eddie to walk a few metres and was so pleased with him when he made it all the way to the door.

Each day of her holiday Emily went back to the farm to spend some time with Eddie.

She took Lucy and Treacle too and positioned them ten metres apart, asking them to sit and wait, so Eddie would look forward to another friendly greeting every time he walked to either one of the dogs or all the way to Emily.

By putting a small gate up into the food stalls Eddie wasn't able to eat all day any more. Instead he would just have his three meals a day, which was more than enough, and within weeks of Emily coming home Eddie was walking over one kilometre each

day. He began to feel so much better and discovered some new parts of the farm that he hadn't been to before. He even made some new friends. He liked talking to the chickens, ducks and Reggie the ram who lived in the furthest field away from his barn.

One day Emily didn't come but Eddie got up anyway and went for his walk which was now over two kilometres. It was a bitterly cold day so Eddie walked quickly to keep warm. As he walked back into the barn the farmer took a photo of him and sent it to Emily.

It was Christmas day, and it was the best Christmas present Emily had that year. She was so pleased to see that Eddie was enjoying his walks and now he was able to go by himself, chatting to new friends on the way.

Emily loved visiting every day until she went back to university. She saw, with tears in her eyes, how much Eddie was improving. She was so proud of him keeping to his new routine and it was obvious that Eddie was chuffed with himself too.

Printed in Great Britain
by Amazon

74713330R00020